JAN 1 4

Text copyright © 2009 by Ken Kimura.
Illustrations copyright © 2009 by Yasunari Murakami.
English translation copyright © 2013 by NorthSouth Books Inc., New York 10016.

First published in Japan in 2009 by Child Honsha Co., Ltd. under the title *999-hiki no kyôdai no Harudesuyo*.
First published in the United States and Canada in 2012 by NorthSouth Books Inc.,
an imprint of NordSüd Verlag AG, CH-8005 Zürich, Switzerland.
English language translation rights arranged with Child Honsha Co., Ltd through Japan Foreign-Rights Centre.
Distributed in the United States by NorthSouth Books Inc., New York 10016.

Library of Congress Cataloging-in-Publication Data is available.
Printed in Germany by Grafisches Centrum Cuno GmbH & Co. KG, 39240 Calbe, October 2012.
ISBN: 978-0-7358-4108-6

1 3 5 7 9 · 10 8 6 4 2

www.northsouth.com

FSC
www.fsc.org
MIX
Paper from
responsible sources
FSC® C043106

999
FROGS
WAKE UP

by Ken Kimura · illustrated by Yasunari Murakami

North
South

Spring had arrived.

Mother Frog was the first to wake up.

She called her froglets. "It's spring! Wake up, everyone!"

One froglet after the other poked its head out of the ground.

POP! POP! POP!

There were 999 brothers and sisters.

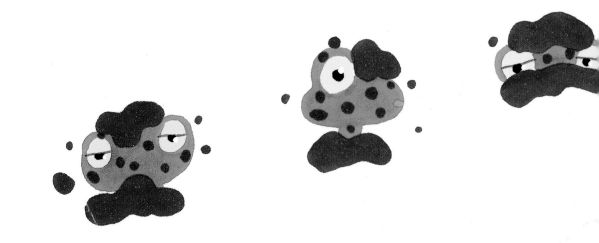

"One, two, three . . . ," Mother Frog counted.

But no matter how many times she counted, she could only find 998 froglets.

"That's strange . . . ," she said.

Then suddenly, the sound of snoring caught her ear.

"Zzz . . . zzz . . . zzz!"

"It's your big brother!" called Mother Frog. "He's still asleep!"
"What a sleepyhead!" said the froglets with a giggle.

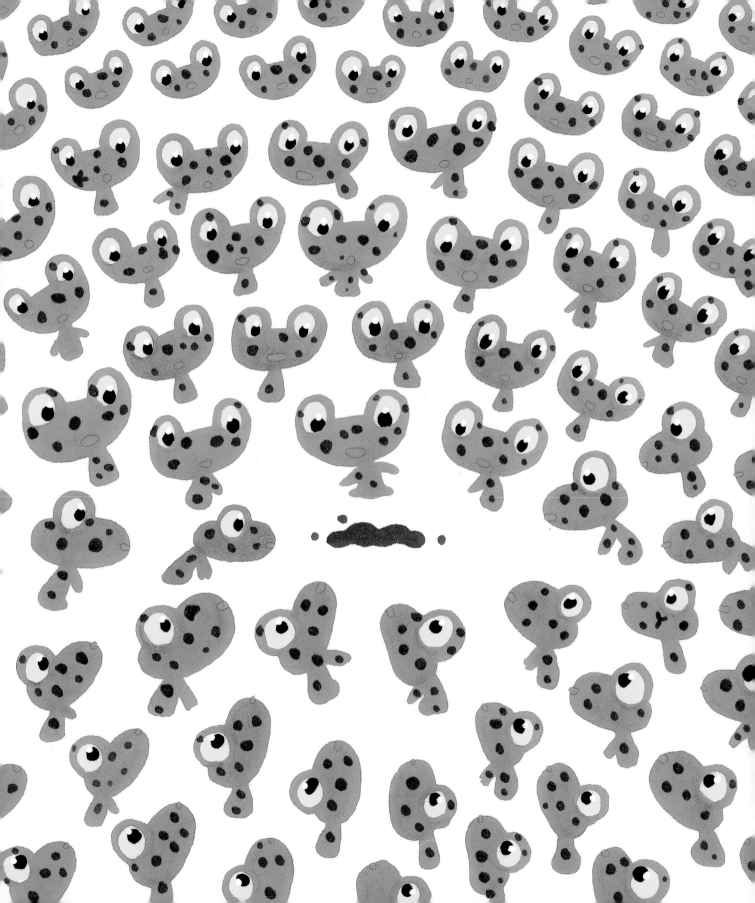

Mother Frog called out to big brother, "Wake up, sleepyhead!"

Big brother finally woke up.

"Good morning, big brother," said Mother Frog and the froglets.

"Oh . . . oh, hi . . . good morning," said big brother, still a little sleepy.

Just then they heard snoring again.

"Zzz . . . zzz . . . zzz!"

"Who is that?" they cried. "Someone else is still sleeping."

"I'll wake him up," said big brother. "Hey, sleepyhead!
It's time to wake up!"

"W . . . what happened?" said a low voice. Then suddenly, an old turtle popped his head out of the ground and asked, "Did I miss spring again?"

"No! The cherry trees are just blossoming," answered the froglets.

The old turtle looked up at the blossoming cherry tree and said, "Oh, it's so beautiful! I always oversleep and miss seeing the flowers, but this year I am awake on time. Thank you!"

Big brother was happy to hear the turtle's words.

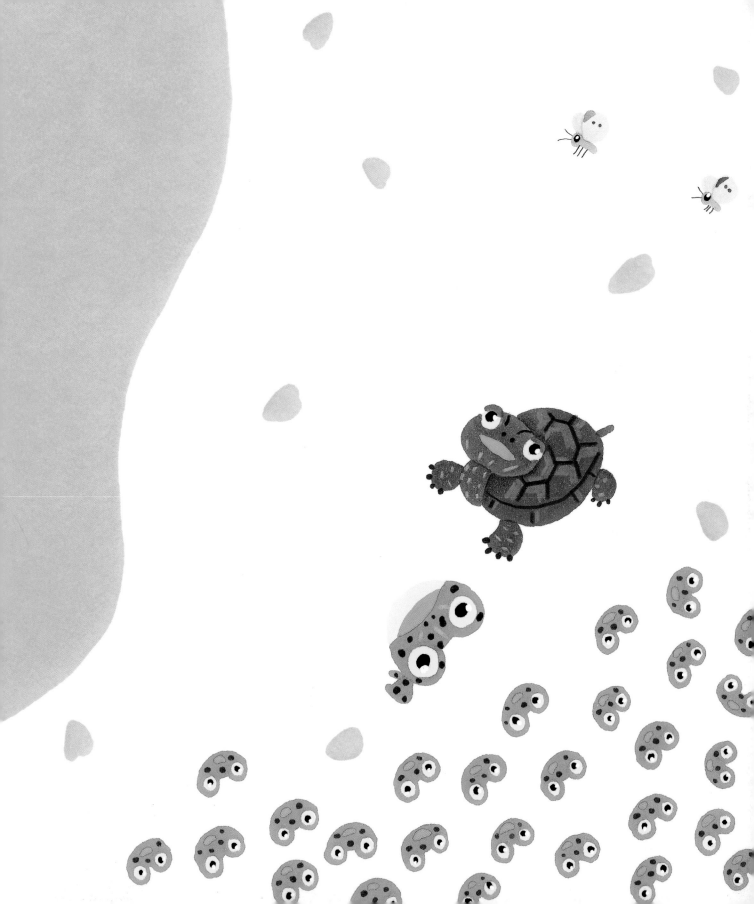

Just then the froglets said, "Over here! It's another sleepyhead!"

"Who could that be?" asked big brother.

He lifted the stone and saw a lizard sleeping soundly.

"What a sleepy lizard," said big brother. "Wake up! It's springtime now!"

The lizard woke up and climbed onto a stone.

"Oh, I feel the warmth on my stomach. Surely spring has arrived," she said dreamily, closing her eyes.

The 999 brothers and sisters closed their eyes for a moment as well.

Then Big brother said, "I have an idea! Let's find more sleepyheads!"

"Yes! Let's go looking!" said the younger brothers and sisters.

"Over here, big brother! There are lots of sleepyheads under these leaves!" called the froglets.

Big brother lifted the leaves and saw ladybugs sleeping all together.

"That's a lot of sleepyheads!" he said.

"Wake up! Spring is here!" called the froglets in chorus.

The ladybugs began to wiggle and wake up.

"Spring is here!"

"I'm hungry!"

"Have the flowers blossomed yet?"

"The aphids in the flowering fields are delicious."

"Let's go and see."

The ladybugs flew away in search of flowers.

The 999 brothers and sisters kept looking, calling, "Sleepyheads, where are you?"

Suddenly, they heard a loud snoring.

"Zzz . . . zzz . . . PHEW . . . zzz . . ."

"Over here! The sleepyhead must be in this hole!" said big brother.

"Wake up, sleepyhead!" he called.

But the sleepyhead would not wake up.

"Zzz . . . zzz . . . phew . . . zzz . . ."

"This is a very tired sleepyhead," said big brother. Then he climbed down into the hole and pulled him, saying, "You must wake up now!"

But the sleepyhead kept sleeping.

"Zzz . . . zzz . . . phew . . . zzz . . ."

Big brother was getting upset.

"Let's pull him out of his hole!"

"Yeah!" shouted the froglets.

They all helped their big brother pull.

"Heave-ho! Heave-ho! Heave-ho!" they cried.

POP!

"It's a big snake!" cried the
999 brothers and sisters.

Mother Frog heard the cry of her froglets. She saw them standing perfectly still in front of the sleepy snake. Big brother trembled, remembering how a snake had chased him last year.

Soon the snake woke up and said, "Hmmm . . . is it time for a nice meal?"

"Not yet, you can sleep some more. We'll wake you when your breakfast is ready," said Mother Frog as gently as if she were soothing a baby.

Then the snake coiled up and went back to sleep.

"Zzz . . . zzz . . . PHEW . . ."

"Psst! Let me help you! You woke me up in time for spring. As a thank-you, I will take the snake deep into the woods," the old turtle whispered, and walked away carrying the snake on his back . . . slowly . . . very slowly.

"That was close! What a relief!" said the 999 brothers and sisters jumping for joy again and again.

"Okay, everyone, make a line," said Mother Frog. "I want to be sure that everyone is safe."

Mother Frog began to count her froglets again. "One, two, three, four, five . . . Uh, oh! Don't move."

But no matter how many times she counted, she could only find 998 froglets.

Big brother was missing.

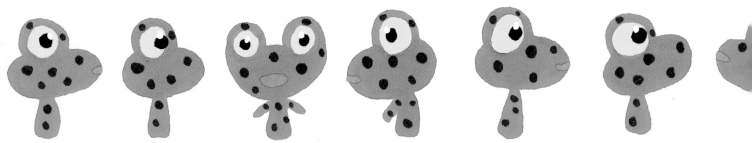

Big brother was just taking a nap.

"Zzz . . . zzz . . . zzz! . . .
Zzz . . . zzz . . . zzz . . ."

It had been a very busy morning.